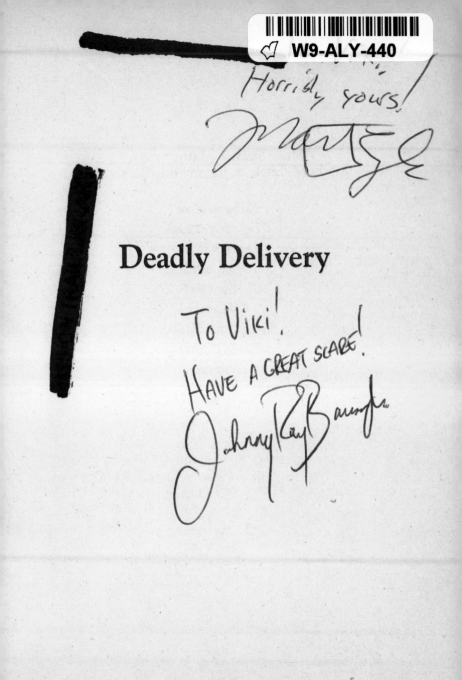

Horridly yours!

Deadly Delivery

To Viki!
Have a great scare!

Johnny Ray Barrington

More **Strange Matter**™ from
Marty M. Engle & Johnny Ray Barnes, Jr.

No Substitutions
The Midnight Game
Driven to Death
A Place to Hide
The Last One In
Bad Circuits
Fly the Unfriendly Skies
Deadly Delivery
Knightmare

Deadly Delivery

Marty M. Engle

A
MONTAGE
PUBLICATION

Montage Publications, a Front Line company,
San Diego, California

TO DOC

There's one in every town.

Some are tall, leaning relics perched high on wind-blown hills. Others squat on barren streets like hollow shells of grey wood and broken glass.

From deserted lighthouses on shrouded shorelines, to empty, stone towers in long-dead fields, they lure the curious in with hushed secrets.

They know stories so dreadful and terrifying that if you heard them, they would freeze your blood or turn your hair snow white.

All over the world, they wait patiently, ready to catch unwary visitors, never to release them again.

Haunted houses.

I have a terrifying story about a haunted

house at 331 Sycamore Street in Fairfield.

My house.

It's a nice, beige, three bedroom in a quiet cul-de-sac with towering trees overhanging a huge backyard, and a leaf-filled tarp covering a pool.

It all started one rainy, stormy night in October as I hurriedly finished yet another award-winning cartoon. Sitting at the cluttered desk in my room, I sketched and drew, wiping away the eraser dust from another masterpiece.

This one turned out awesome.

Wait! One final touch. I pushed the pencil across the rounded head, swirling and swirling in a gentle arc until a perfect nest of hair sat on top of my prize creation, COOL DOG YAK! My absolute best character, and the subject of an ongoing, underground success story with my closest friends at Fairfield Junior High, seventh grade.

He's got a hot dog body, simple face, and stick arms and legs: crude but effective. His speciality is mocking teachers and destroying a cartoon version of the infamous Kyle Banner in gross and disgusting ways.

That's what made my strip so popular

with my friends. They all love seeing Kyle get his. But he deserves it for all the terror he dishes out. I'm talking about rubber band welts the size of golf balls, books drop-kicked out of three-story windows, and humiliating public thrashings for reasons unknown.

COOL DOG YAK stands up for what's right and gives Kyle exactly what he deserves. Something I sure wished *I* could do.

I've always been afraid of Kyle, as long as I can remember. It's not just that he could beat me up, it's that everyone would *watch* him beat me up. I have a real problem with being the center of attention. Good or bad. I always think I'll screw up or choke or something. I prefer to stay on the sidelines and be nice and quiet.

Anyway, my friends think I draw Kyle perfectly; that I have him down to a science.

It's no wonder.

He lives next door.

I ran to the wall and pinned my latest and greatest up with the rest of my cartoons.

Glancing through my curtain and the rain to the house next door, I didn't see any sign of movement from Kyle's bedroom window.

I knew the chance of Kyle seeing those

drawings from his window was remote, but I could never be too careful. As far as I knew, he hasn't even heard about them.

Naturally, none of my friends have told Kyle, or shown him the cartoons. They've been extra careful to keep it an absolute secret, ensuring my safety and their entertainment. I didn't want to think about what would happen if he ever saw one of my cartoons. They'd probably never find my body.

"SIMON! MOM'S ON THE PHONE!" Sarah yelled from downstairs.

Sarah is my twin sister. She helps me pass the cartoons out in class to the select viewers, at extreme risk to her own life. Kyle acknowledges no difference between boys and girls, only that they should fear him equally.

Sarah could probably talk her way out of a thrashing if she had to. She's a great talker and reader, and always gets the highest scores in oral reports. She's kind of a brain, but everyone likes her because she's so nice all the time. She's almost *too* nice.

We look so much alike, it creeps some people out. Because of our super bright-blue eyes and white-blond hair, people tell us we look like dolls. They treat us like we're mind-linked or something.

"SIMON!" Sarah yelled again.

"WHAT DOES SHE WANT?" I yelled back, hanging out my bedroom door.

"SHE WANTS TO TALK TO YOU!"

Great. Mom and Dad had gone over to the Donaldson's about three hours before. They always wound up going to somebody's house on Friday nights. "We'll be back by nine," Mom said. It now was ten-thirty.

I bounced down the steps and saw the phone hanging on its stand in the foyer.

"Why'd you hang up?" I yelled, noticing the rain outside had really started to come down. I could see sheets of water running down the frosted glass windows that framed the front door.

"Mom had to go. She just wanted us to know they were going to be very late," Sarah said, stepping in from the living room.

She was still holding her prized journal. That little diary held every thought, every secret, every hope she had. She carried it around everywhere and wrote in it every day. It's practically her best friend.

"Should we ground them?" I joked.

"You'll definitely want to. She said Ms. Glower's coming over in an hour."

"WHAT! Oh, no. WHY? We're too big for a sitter. How old does she think we are? We're not babies! We can take care of ourselves!"

A crack of lightning flashed outside.

The lights flickered and dimmed, then sputtered back on.

"Uh, oh. The power's going to go," Sarah said, peering up at the domed light in the hallway ceiling.

"Yeah, maybe. So what? We're twelve years old, for Pete's sake! Why did Mom go and do that?"

Another crack of lightning flashed, followed by a thundering boom that sounded like it came from just outside the door, startling us, making us jump.

"Whoa. Did you feel that?" Sarah asked, her eyes widening.

"Yeah. So what? It's just a stupid storm. I'll get the flashlight if the power goes out."

"I'm just glad Ms. Glower will be here soon," Sarah muttered, obviously comforted by the thought.

"Oh, give me a break. Not you, too! We are perfectly capable of staying alone."

The rain pounded hard on the roof of the house. The lights flickered again as a shrieking wind rattled the windows in their frames.

"We know all the routines! The police number, the fire number, the number of the neighbors," I ranted, waving my arms about. "Don't do this. Don't do that. Don't talk on the phone if there's lightning outside."

The rain fell harder, in heavy sheets.

"Don't stand too close to windows if the wind is blowing too hard."

The wind blew stronger, whipping against the windows with a shrill whistle.

"And the ever popular: Don't open the door to strangers."

The doorbell rang.

I stopped my ranting. We looked at the door, stunned, as if the bell had chimed on cue.

The doorbell rang again.

"No way," I whispered.

"Who? Ms. Glower?" Sarah asked.

We froze in place. No way Ms. Glower could have gotten over here this fast if Mom had just called her. We both knew it.

"I don't think so," I gulped.

The doorbell rang again as a deafening clap of thunder shook the house.

The lights blew out, plunging us into total darkness.

My heart nearly flew from my chest. Sarah gasped, clutching me. "Simon, the window! Look!"

Another flash of lightning lit the skinny windows beside the door, revealing the huge, hulking shape of a man, right outside the door, swaying back and forth . . .

trying to peer inside.

The doorbell rang again.

We froze in place as the dark shape rocked in front of the window, our eyes following every shuffle with nervous disbelief.

Sarah squeezed my shoulder as three taps sounded from behind the door.

Neither of us moved a muscle.

"Should we see who it is?" Sarah whispered through the darkness.

My eyes stared unblinking at the front door, waiting nervously for the next sign of movement. "Why? I don't want to know."

Sarah's voice shifted behind me, growing harsher than before. "Okay, Mister Brave. You're the one who doesn't need a sitter. Now see who it is!"

"Are you nuts? As far as I'm concerned, we're not even home. Got it?"

As if in reply, three more taps sounded against the door.

"Whoever it is knows we're in here. Look through the peephole, at least." Sarah shoved me toward the door with a quick thrust.

I turned and glared angrily in her direction. I could make out her outline, waving me forward silently .

"Okay! Okay," I whispered gruffly.

Three loud knocks quickened my pulse as I leaned toward the door, my eyes squinting with each rap.

I carefully placed my fingers on the wood, and eased my eye to the peephole.

A burst of lightning lit the side of a scarred, mangled face, leaning into the peephole, *peering back!* A red, twisted mouth stretched tight over gnarled teeth, shiny black eyes glistened from beneath a weathered cap.

My whole body stiffened as a swell of dread surged in my stomach. No way! A lunatic! Unbelievable! A raving lunatic at our door, on the one stupid night we were home alone.

"HAllooooo," the voice cracked dryly. "Anyone there?"

I jerked away, startled and shaken, backing

into Sarah.

"Who is it? What'd he look like?"

"You don't want to know."

The steady stream of knocks continued, growing louder and heavier by the second.

"He's not going to go away," Sarah choked, grabbing my arm and holding tightly.

The knocks grew into pounding, and the pounding into hammering!

He was going to bust the door in!

"Should I call the p-p-police?" I stammered, stumbling backward.

Sarah drew a long breath, preparing to scream, when the hammering stopped.

A sudden, heavy thud slammed the bottom of the door.

Then silence, only the wind and the heavy sheets of rain blowing against the house.

We backed away from the door, into the dark hallway, our eyes scanning the windows for movement.

"He kicked the door," Sarah gasped.

"No. Maybe he fell. He looked like he had been in a car wreck."

Lightning crashed as a car engine roared to life in the driveway. I heard the squeal of tires as a brilliant light shone through the windows around the door.

I ran to the door and peered out the slim window beside it. A large, white vehicle, headlights blazing, sped around the circle of our cul-de-sac, heading toward the street.

I grabbed the doorknob and unhooked the door latch. It had to be that weirdo getting away, taking off down the street.

"Simon! WAIT! NO!" Sarah yelled.

"It was him! In the van! It had to be!" I jerked the door open, hoping to get a better look at our mysterious visitor.

What I got was the surprise of my life.

A box was propped against the door. I nearly tripped over it as I ran out. It was a white, cardboard box about four feet long and three feet high, wrapped tightly in clear plastic, beaded with rainwater.

"Look!" I shouted, pointing to the end of the street.

A white van, stamped with large, black and red lettering turned the corner and sped away in the rain.

"A delivery man! Man, I feel like an idiot!" I groaned and turned back around, smacking my own stupid forehead for acting like such a baby.

"What a relief," Sarah exhaled loudly from the doorway. "I thought he would bust in here for sure. Hey, you know . . . we should call his company or something. He scared us to death! He didn't say who he was or anything. They shouldn't be allowed to pound like that. We could get him fired. He *deserves* it . . . " Sarah fumed on and on. It was not like her at all. I don't think I had ever seen her so mad.

"We acted like we weren't here, remember? He had to make sure no one was around, right? For a delivery this late, it *has* to be important." Yeah. Important. Cool.

I knelt down, searching over the top and sides of the box excitedly. We rarely got a delivery, so this was a major event, and this late? . . . There could be anything in the box.

"No address. I wonder if he got the wrong house?" Sarah muttered, kneeling to join me, running her fingers along the edges.

"I don't know. Who cares. It's ours now. Let's get it inside!"

I slowly dragged the kitchen knife across the tape holding the cardboard flaps together, following the seam. "Ahhh, a perfect incision." I handed the knife to Nurse Sarah, pushing my wet hair from my face.

With a tug and a tear, a strand of tape fluttered down to join the pile of plastic wrap in the middle of the living room. We sat on our knees as close to the precious package as possible.

The flaps, in their new-found freedom, popped up, offering a tempting peek inside at the mysterious contents of the box.

"Wait, Simon. How do we even know if this box made it to the right house? Isn't it a federal offense to open someone else's mail? I don't want to go to jail over something so stupid. MAJOR permanent record *scar*."

"Get outta here! I could totally see us on America's Most Wanted, hands behind our backs, our faces all blocked out with a computer blur. The announcer going, *"They* opened mail they shouldn't have. Your calls helped bring them to justice . . . tonight on . . .""

Sarah punched me in the side.

"OW! Okay, okay. Anyway, they dropped it off here. That means it's *ours* now. *OURS! DO YOU HEAR? OURS! HA ha ha ha ha ha!"* I gave my best maniacal laugh. The same laugh I gave when I would send Kyle Banner to a hideous dooK m in one of my comic strips.

I jerked the flaps open, anxiously peering inside to find . . .

a trunk.

"A trunk?" My excitement deflated immediately.

"An old trunk," Sarah said, her eyes lit with amazement.

"What, like from the fifties?"

"Like from the thirteenth century."

Now *she* was the one getting excited. Sarah loves history and geography and all that stuff. Most of her favorite shows are on the Discovery Channel. She has all of them taped and cataloged.

"Okay, Braniac, so it's an *old* trunk. What a rip." I couldn't believe it. I didn't know what I wanted to find, but it sure wasn't a trunk. Still, I wondered what could be inside.

It filled the box. An old piece of luggage: dark olive green, with cracked leather straps and handles. I could see the tops of tarnished locks and latches. Most of all I could . . .

"Whoa! This thing stinks!" I cried, waving my hands in front of my face. "It smells like the bottom of your closet."

"HEY!" Sarah cried out, punching my side with her tiny, white fist. She couldn't punch her way out of a soggy sack if she tried.

"It's an antique. You should show more

respect. We have no idea where it came from. Where it was going. It's history . . ."

"Yeah, yeah. Lets pry it open."

"You can't just yank it out and claw it open, doofus. Look at it! It could fall apart."

I plunged my arms into the box. "Bah, they made trunks *better* in the old days. Help me out," I grunted, grabbing the side handle.

Sarah sighed and in a few moments we placed the single ugliest piece of luggage ever created onto the living room floor.

"Want to do the honors?" I asked, presenting the kitchen knife across my arm like a sword.

"It's not even locked, brain-drain," Sarah laughed, opening the latches.

Her fingers slid across the large, central latch, flipped it and stopped.

"You open it," she muttered.

She chickened out. I knew she would. Sarah gets scared really easily. If she gets really scared, she curls up into a ball and whimpers. What a chicken.

"No problem," I remarked calmly, grabbing the lid and flinging it back.

An explosion of light knocked us back five feet, and flat onto the floor.

A tremendous column of light surged up like a fountain from the trunk, snaking and twisting through the air.

Our eyes, wide with shock, watched as the stream of light struck the ceiling and sprayed down in a shower.

A loud sound, like a tremendous wind, swept through the room and made my ears pop. I felt a weird pressure in my head, and a strange tingling made every muscle in my body twitch.

The trunk seemed washed out, faded, as did everything else in the room. The light made it very difficult to see. I had the vague impression that something was moving through the light, racing around the ceiling, swooping in a figure eight.

"DO YOU SEE IT?" Sarah yelled.

The shape rushed from the ceiling, straight at me!

I threw my hands up in front of my face, afraid it would smack into me.

A groan escaped my mouth as I saw two hideous, gleaming eyes peering through my fingers, floating in the middle of a vague, swirling form.

The loud, cloudy form flew away from my shaking body with a hideous laugh, and disappeared into the wall, sucking the light along with it.

"LOOK!" Sarah cried.

We watched from the floor as the splotch of light rushed down the living room wall, *from the inside.*

It looked as if it were scurrying *behind* our walls, like a screaming, waving ball of light. Mom's favorite painting fell from the wall as the light passed behind it.

I watched with a mixed sense of amazement and dread as the light disappeared around the corner that led to the hallway and kitchen.

The lid on the trunk dropped down with a slam and the latches closed, all by themselves.

I swallowed hard.

"WHAT DID YOU LET LOOSE IN OUR HOUSE?" Sarah yelled.

"HOW WAS I SUPPOSED TO KNOW?"

We ran to the corner and looked quickly around, fear gnawing at my insides. I almost didn't *want* to find it.

No trace of it. Not on the stairs. Not in the hall. The front door was still closed and sheets of rain still pounded against the windows.

No sign of it anywhere.

The lights flickered, then suddenly the power came back on.

"W-what was that thing?" I stammered, my eyes darting around for any sign of movement.

We yelped and jumped as we heard a crash in the kitchen.

"What do you mean *was? It's still here!* You let a ghost loose in the house!"

A huge crash from the kitchen, like a tornado sweeping through or a bomb exploding. Either way, it sounded like disaster.

I peeked carefully around the corner from the hallway, Sarah right behind me.

The cabinets were all open. The plates and cups and glasses, once inside, now lay on the floor in a zillion pieces.

The chairs around the kitchen table had been turned upside down and thrown across the floor.

The refrigerator door swayed slightly, almost pointing to the cooking island in the center of the room. All the food from the 'fridge sat stacked like a dripping tower on the stove.

"Oh, no," I muttered.

The stove underneath the pile of food had

been turned on! All the cooking eyes glowed red hot. A small waft of smoke drifted up from a blackening milk carton.

Tupperware with grisly leftovers melted and bubbled. Large, fat drips of yogurt hissed and curdled on the glowing rings.

The ceiling dripped with broken eggs, ketchup splotches and Creamy Ranch dressing, the empty containers scattered on the floor.

I moaned softly and pulled back into the hallway, crouching down next to Sarah. I didn't have to say anything. My face said it all.

"The ghost wrecked our kitchen. Right?" Sarah said, trembling.

"We don't know for sure *what* it is, but yes. . . It destroyed our kitchen. What are we going to do? Mom and Dad are going to see this mess and auction us off, or something!"

I stewed a moment more. "Come on, let's go."

"Are you crazy? I'm not going in there! We have to get out of here! We have to call the police!" I stopped her as she rose to leave.

"And tell them what? We don't even know what it is. I have to turn the stove off before the whole kitchen catches on fire. Now come on!"

"No way!" Sarah answered.

"Please? I need you to watch out for me. Okay? Please?" I pleaded.

"I'm going to regret this," she reluctantly answered.

I crept carefully into the kitchen, glass and bits of ceramic crunching with each step.

The lights above flickered on and off erratically. Sarah followed right behind, guarding my back, as I made my way to the stove in the center of the room . . .

and carefully turned the dials to off.

"Simon, look," Sarah whispered, pointing to the counter on the left wall.

Mom's entire collection of gourmet coffee had been moved from the glass cabinet above. It was now stacked in neat rows along the counter, each small paper bag puckering open at the top.

"What now?" I asked.

The paper bags tilted downward, like cannons, the mouths of the bags opening wider. "How?" I managed to say before . . .

The coffee beans shot out of the bags, hosing us in a thick spray! The air clogged with the beans as they flew around us like a dark cloud of angry bees. We cried out, covering our heads with our arms, protecting our eyes from the stinging, bullet-like barrage.

The last of them hurtled past.

Sarah screamed at the sight as the beans hit the wall and stuck there . . .
forming two words!

HOLD STILL!

"Huh?" I uttered in astonishment, sensing someone beside me.

I turned and saw it.

A blue, terrifying form hovered over the counter near the empty 'fridge. Its eyes blazed crazily inside its baggy, cloudy form. Two long, hideous hands stretched out . . .

and grabbed the knives from the wooden knife block.

"WAIT! NO!" I yelled.

The knives circled his body swiftly, until they became a blur. His terrible cackling seemed to speed them along, sending them flying out, straight at us!

We jumped behind the center island as the deadly blades whizzed over our heads! I heard several loud THWACKS as the rest buried themselves in the wooden side of the center island . . . where we had been standing mere moments before.

"HE'S TRYING TO KILL US!" Sarah screamed.

The loud, cackling laugh whooshed past the island in a flash, out into the hallway, and up the stairs.

We popped up and glanced around, double checking for any further sign of the little terror.

I heard the upstairs hall table fall over, then the shattering of a vase.

"If he wanted to kill us, he wouldn't have missed. He didn't have to warn us! He's *playing* with us, trying to *scare* us," I said, growing angrier by the moment.

"It worked! He did a great job. BRAVO! I'm leaving now," Sarah started for the hallway again.

Then I noticed the light on in the oven.

So did Sarah.

"What? No. NO! NOOOOO!" she cried.

Sarah slammed the kitchen drawer shut, slid on an oven mitt, and fished the charred, crispy remains of her prized *journal* out of the oven which had been set to broil.

"Ewwww." The only word to describe the blackened mess.

I saw a fire burning in Sarah's eyes. A fire I had never seen before. For the first time, she looked furious beyond all reason. Angry beyond all description.

While holding the charred remains of her best friend, her lips curled up, and her eyes narrowed.

"Now it's personal," she snarled.

We crept silently to the top of the stairs. The shattered remains of a vase sprinkled the last three steps. We carefully avoided stepping on any of the pieces.

I raised a finger to my mouth, motioning for silence as we stepped around the overturned hall table.

I looked down the hall to the left, toward Mom and Dad's room. The hall lights flickered on and off as another crack of thunder boomed outside. No sign of the little monster, only framed pictures and striped wall paper.

I looked down the hall to the right. Sarah's room, the first door to the right, seemed undisturbed. My room, the first door to the left, also seemed quiet.

Sarah squeezed my arm and pointed past

the linen closets to the end of the hall, past our rooms.

The bathroom door opened very slowly and very slightly.

The lights dimmed and hissed as a tremendous burst of lightning lit the entryway at the bottom of the stairs.

"He's gotta be in there," I mouthed silently to Sarah. She still quivered with anger from the loss of her best friend, her journal.

"Let's get him," she growled.

Slowly we crept down the hallway.

As we continued along, I kept trying to form a firm mental picture of what the little creep looked like. It was hard, because he almost seemed to change form from moment to moment, like smoke in the air. The only permanent feature seemed to be the eyes. He had huge, bulging eyes that stared out at us, unblinking.

His mouth spread as wide as his head, full of tiny, sharp teeth, but a moment later it could shrink to be as small and puckery as a bow tie.

His bulbous and twisted nose seemed way too small for his head. It sat *between* his eyes, just over the mouth.

His body seemed tiny to nonexistent. Scrawny, tapering arms and long, bony hands waved about him as he flew. Pretty ugly, even for a ghost, if that's what he was.

I looked through the crack in the door into the bathroom. No light. No noise.

"What do we do if we catch him?" I whispered.

Sarah fixed me with a fierce stare and said, "Let's find him first."

The bathroom door slowly swung open to the inside. Light from the hall spread across the wall mirror to the left, just above the sink. The toilet lid was down, the small rug near the tub undisturbed.

The shower curtain had been pulled shut; a dark, striped print that we couldn't see through.

I froze and studied it, watching for any movement, any sign of anything that could be hiding behind it. No bumps or bulges. No stirs or shuffles.

I turned and mouthed to Sarah, "Should we turn on the lights?"

She shook her head and signalled me forward. HA! Easy for her to say. Brave as she had gotten, I still wound up in front.

I crept to the shower curtain with my hand raised up, ready to throw it open. My heart raced. I felt tiny needles of dread pricking my neck. It was the kind of silence where you can hear every sound your body makes; breathing, swallowing. Sarah bumped me lightly from behind. I could practically hear her heart thumping in her chest.

From the corner of my eye, I saw our reflections in the mirror and the reflection of the shower curtain.

I steadied myself, then threw the shower curtain open!

Nothing.

The door behind us SLAMMED SHUT, pushed closed by a large, bony hand. The ghost emerged from the wall behind the door. Its eyes shone like headlights. It rushed forward, shrieking and laughing, "TONIGHT'S THE NIGHT!"

We screamed and stumbled back, tripping over the rug, falling into the shower. Somehow, I hit the water knob and the shower sprang on, spraying out everywhere and drenching us!

The ghost suddenly recoiled, a horrified look on its face. Its eyes grew wide and its pupils shrank. Its mouth curled up into a sneer and it plunged through the door, escaping down the hall, scraping the walls with its long hands.

I turned the water off, gasping and choking. "Well, it sure doesn't like water! COME ON! LET'S GO!"

We scrambled out of the tub, threw open the bathroom door and bolted into the hallway. Sarah stopped with a jerk.

"Simon! LOOK!" Sarah blurted, coughing and pointing as the vaporous form plunged through the door . . .

INTO MY ROOM!

I ran into my room, expecting the worst.
I wasn't disappointed. The thing had completely
trashed my room, *in a matter of seconds!*

All my clothes sat tied together in a huge
knot in the middle of my overturned bed. A perfect
ball! How did he do that?

My collectable cartoon posters, from classic
Looney Tunes to AAAHH! Real Monsters, drifted
through the air in shredded strips.

The wallpaper, ripped and torn, rolled
and unrolled down the walls like yo-yos.

My window, thrown wide open, allowed
sheets of rain to puddle on my carpet.

Then I saw him, floating in front of the
corkboard with my COOL DOG YAK cartoons!
The only things left intact.

"NOOOOO!" I cried as he glared over at

me, before he smiled and plunged into the cork-board with a flash!

My eyes desperately darted from cartoon to cartoon, looking for any sign of the ghastly ghost.

There was the one where COOL DOG runs Kyle Banner over with a steamroller.

Nothing.

There was the one where COOL DOG crams Kyle Banner into a garbage compactor, head first.

Nothing.

Then I looked at the one where COOL DOG flushes Kyle Banner down a toilet.

Nothing.

Then I came to the one where COOL DOG sticks Kyle Banner in a microwave oven.

I watched with horror as COOL DOG moved on the paper!

Impossible! He actually, physically moved on the paper!

He reached over *in the drawing,* to the microwave oven with Kyle Banner's cartoon face peering out pitifully, crying for help.

He put Kyle on three minutes and pressed start!

"NOOOOO!" I cried out, grabbing the paper off the corkboard and wadding it up.

I looked up in time to see COOL DOG grabbing up a giant fly swatter in another cartoon! He raised it over a bug with Kyle Banner's face! The bug screamed pitifully for its life.

"NO!" I yelled, grabbing *that* cartoon and wadding it up.

One after another, the cartoons came to life, each about to put an end to poor Kyle Banner in terrible ways!

All my fault! It was funny before, but it didn't seem funny now. Sweat beaded on my forehead as I struggled, grabbing papers off the corkboard left and right! I tried to keep up, but couldn't. One after another, high-pitched, pitiful cries of doom rose from the papers, rustling and shaking on the corkboard. All calling my name, begging for my help!

"STOP IT! STOP IT!" I cried, then froze as the cartoon in my hand *changed*.

COOL DOG stopped and looked up, straight at me, and in a dry, cracked voice muttered, **"THESE ARE FAR TOO GOOD TO KEEP TO YOURSELF!"**

The pins in the corkboard shook and twisted, then flew off! I cried out, knocking the stinging little tacks away as my cartoons flew from the wall and swirled through the air around me.

Sarah grabbed me and pulled me aside as the entire board flew off the wall and cracked on the ground.

"LOOK!" She cried.

I couldn't breathe. I couldn't yell. I couldn't

believe it! No fate could have been worse. He had tapped into my absolute worst fear and brought it to life.

The cartoons sailed out my window, and flew in a straight line . . . *to Kyle Banner's slowly opening window next door.*

7

I flew down the stairs, jumping the last few steps, and jerked the front door open.

Sarah peered down from the top of the stairs, yelling behind me, "SIMON! WAIT!"

Lightning cracked through the dark, churning sky. The houses looked like faint, blue outlines in the rain.

I had to get those cartoons back! If Kyle saw them, I might as well move to another country, and even then he would track me down. I had to get them back!

It wouldn't stop with just one reminder. Oh, no. Each time he saw me, he would remind me of my grave error in mocking him. I could look forward to the traditional Kyle Banner method: torn clothes, a black eye and public humiliation.

The rain pounded the top of my head, and

I could barely make out the outline of the steps leading to the Banner's door. I saw the little metal numbers 333 hanging on the door frame.

"Lousy ghost," I mumbled.

Trembling, I rang the bell and hoped.

I heard someone swear, curse and stomp across the floor, coming right to the . . .

"**WHAT DO YOU WANT?**" The angry voice barked down as the door flung open.

Kyle stood in a torn flannel shirt, dirty grey sweatpants and tube socks that flopped out awkwardly, like a clown's shoes.

"I . . . I . . ." I couldn't look away from the fiery red patch of hair that stood straight up from his thin, yellowed scalp.

"What do you WANT, White? I'm trying to get to the Icon of Evil, level 30 before the power goes out again," he snarled.

Behind him in the living room, across a minefield of frozen pizza boxes and tangled control wires, the television blared away. The screen paused on the game **DOOM**, Kyle's favorite.

"I . . . I . . ." *Think, stupid.* He hasn't been upstairs, yet. He doesn't know. Say something! You have to get those cartoons, before he finds them, I told myself. I was blowing it. BLOWING IT!

"Did the big, bad storm scare you? Did you want someone to hold your hand? . . . **OR DO YOU HAVE SOME KIND OF DEATH WISH OR SOMETHING?**" He grabbed my collar and nearly pulled me off the ground.

"I-It's just . . . I-I was w-wondering. . ."

NO! Behind him, at the top of the staircase, the ghost flew into sight, pinning the cartoons on the wall, lining the hallways, whistling to himself.

"I'm wondering why I'm wasting time talking to you. **NOW BEAT IT!**" He shoved me down the steps to the sidewalk.

"NO! WAIT!" I cried.

The door slammed shut, causing the little, metal house numbers to come loose and hang upside down.

I moaned, my mouth gaping open like a fish. Any minute now. Any time he would go upstairs and that would be that. Finished. That little, lousy ghost practically wallpapered Kyle's house with the cartoons.

I slowly began to trudge through the rain, back toward my house.

I couldn't think fast enough. But what could I have said? "Hi, Kyle! Let me go upstairs and get something out of your room I desperately don't want you to see. Right."

Hopeless. My breath quickened and my pulse started pounding. A seething anger made my face tingle. The rain practically hissed against my red skin.

That little, lousy *thing!* It knew right where to hurt me. It knew, somehow.

Suddenly, I heard a loud whoosh and a laugh that echoed with evil!

I looked across the yard, startled to see a little, blue ball of light with arms flying through the air, out Kyle's window and back into my own! NO! The ghost flew back into my house! Oh, no. In my desperation, I had forgotten . . .

"Sarah!" I cried. I had left her in there alone! What was I thinking!

I ran down the walk as fast as I could.

Just in time to see the bright headlights of a car pull into my driveway . . . *and stop.*

"Hi, Ms. Glower!" I said, as cheerfully as I could fake, running up to meet her on the sidewalk, as she headed toward the house. The rain bounced off the still-warm hood of her car.

Her raincoat made her look huge. Her short, dark hair, heavily sprayed and hard as a football helmet, didn't get wet in the traditional sense of the word. Water sort of beaded on the surface and rolled off. Her pale, puffy face peered at me with motherly concern from under her umbrella.

"SIMON! What on earth are you doing out in the rain? Your mother will be furious at you. You're soaked to the skin."

"I was just . . . taking a walk?" She'd never believe me about the ghost. How could I tell her? What could I say? Still, Sarah could be in danger.

Would she help us? Could she help us? Or was I better off trying to take care of this mess myself? Maybe Sarah was right. I might be in *major* trouble for opening that box in the first place.

I didn't have to think about it for long.

I saw the blue, glowing ghost rise behind her, smiling wildly, eyes blazing.

"Ms. Glower, I . . . I . . ."

I watched in amazement as the ghost smiled and pulled out a huge, glowing hatchet, swinging it high over Ms. Glower's head. It looked at me, as if for approval!

I shook my head, no. Choking, searching for my voice, lost in terror.

"Simon, what's wrong? Is something the matter?" Ms. Glower asked as the ghost put away the hatchet and pulled out a battle axe instead! Double bladed and razor sharp.

"NOOOOOO! Everything's fine. Why do you ask?" I gasped, as the ghost looked at me again for approval, floating in the air behind Ms. Glower. I shook my head, no, vigorously.

"You look as if you've seen a ghost," she muttered, shifting the umbrella from one hand to the other.

The ghost behind her put away the

battle axe and produced a large, glowing sword instead! Lifting it high.

"I don't think so!" I yelled.

The ghost stopped.

It looked disappointed at my objection. It put the sword away, shrugged . . . and tied a ghostly bib around its neck.

"You don't think what?" Ms. Glower asked, confused and growing anxious.

"I don't think . . . you're going to believe what's behind you," I cried, backing slowing away.

Ms. Glower spun around and SCREAMED as the ghost swelled like a balloon, opened its mouth wide and swallowed her whole, *in one gulp!*

I nearly gagged as I watched her fall through the cloudy form, kicking and screaming inside before falling out the bottom with a puff of mist. She gasped for air, her eyes staring crazily, and . . . *her hair snow white.*

Everything after that seemed like a blur. Ms. Glower scrambled to her car, babbling wildly, out of her head from sheer terror.

The ghost laughed and rolled in the air, giggling maniacally while Ms. Glower's car swerved and screeched down the rain-slicked street, her hysterical screams vanishing as she drove out of sight.

All right. Enough was enough.

An explosion of anger rocketed out of my mouth. "ALL RIGHT! LOOK, YOU! I DON'T KNOW WHO YOU ARE OR WHERE YOU THINK YOU ARE, BUT . . ."

It stopped laughing and floated nose to nose with me. Its eyes burned with hate and seemed to stare right through me, but I refused to back down, no matter how scared I really felt.

My blood froze as its voice changed into a far more serious tone.

"I'M HOME," it growled, swishing through the air and into the front door, the draft nearly knocking me down.

A series of bright flashes exploded in the house, like a million flashbulbs going off at once. I could see the lights everywhere, through the curtains and the windows. All over the house! What was he doing? What *could* he be doing? Then a loud, horrible sound, like an explosion.

All the lights suddenly went out. Whatever he had been doing, stopped.

I stood there for a moment, stunned. The full reality of my grim situation really sinking in.

His home, huh?

"W-we'll see about that," I stammered, mounting the steps and pushing through the front door.

What I saw took my breath away.

I stepped inside what *used* to be my home. The ghost wasn't kidding. *Everything had changed.*

My footsteps echoed. It sounded as if I were walking around in a . . .

castle?

The door slammed shut behind me, loudly, solidly, far more heavily than it should have. No wonder. *It wasn't my door anymore.* It was now about ten feet tall and made of thick, old wood laced with iron strips.

"This can't be happening. I only *think* it's happening," I mumbled quietly to myself. I couldn't stop shaking. I felt cold, small. How could this be possible?

The only explanation I could think of chilled me to the bone. The little creep changed my house. He actually *changed* my house. He changed it into *his* house . . .

a haunted castle.

A large, wheel-shaped wooden chandelier dangled from a long chain attached to wooden beams thirty feet above my head. Candles circled the wheel, covered in cobwebs.

I noticed the gently curving stone walls that spread out seventy feet on both sides.

Elaborate tapestries draped down from wooden posts every ten feet along the walls. They showed people in strange armor skewering pigs, burning down huts and torturing what looked like poor farmers.

A tremendous stone staircase spiraled up into the gloom directly ahead, where *our* staircase used to be.

Then I noticed some of the walls had small, bar-covered indentations. Inside them I could see clay pots and metal plates.

An arched doorway led to the left, and another led to the right, each about ten feet high, cobwebs draping the openings like curtains.

Strange metal medallions and crests hung around the room, some gold, some copper. All had a strange, small figure with large eyes.

Large, staring eyes.

Terrible sculptures of misshapen monsters glared at me from stone columns set high in the room.

"T-Terrific. J-Just s-s-swell," I stammered, picking up a candle from a small table near the stairs.

It lit by itself, much to my dismay.

"SAAAARRRRAAAH!" I yelled. My voice echoed loudly in the grand, hollow hall.

No response.

"SARAH?" I yelled again, peering through the dark up the stairs.

Nothing.

I had to decide where to start looking, if I could stop my legs from shaking. This place sure looked big. Far bigger than any house. Well, I guess castles were *supposed* to be big. Big and scary, right? Should I start looking downstairs? Through one of the doorways?

Then a scream from upstairs made my decision for me.

Higher and higher, I climbed the stone steps, the candlelight reaching about ten feet around me. Past that, only pitch-black darkness.

The screaming I had been following suddenly stopped . . . and so did I.

Now I heard a faint sound, like something scurrying over stone. Then low chirps and whistles, like wind through a window.

The candle flickered, threatening to go out as I continued up the stairs. My heart skipped a beat as the flame danced, then settled.

I finally reached the top of the stairs. I couldn't even see down to the bottom anymore.

The upstairs corridor seemed much wider than it was before, when it was the hall of *our* house. Now it had a stone floor with low archways and many narrow doors, at least a dozen, stretching off in both directions.

Spider webs covered everything, and some wooden support beams had fallen into the middle of the hall. I heard a loud creaking and groaning, like straining wood. Everything smelled old and dank.

"Sarah?" I whispered, afraid to yell.

Nothing.

"SARAH?" I said a little louder.

I heard a faint voice, though it was hard to tell where it was coming from. It could have been from *any* of the rooms.

"Siiimmmmon!" The voice called, maybe from the left, toward where our rooms *used* to be. Of course. Sarah was probably in her room. Or where her room *used* to be.

I slowly crept toward the sound of the voice, carefully guarding the flame.

I noticed many small indentions in the walls as I passed. They looked liked windows that had been boarded up. Small shafts of dim light shone through very narrow slits carved in the wood.

Arrow loops, I think they called them. Guards could shoot out, but enemies couldn't shoot in. I remembered seeing a cool show on castles once. Now, I wished I had paid more attention. I think it was on the Discovery Channel. *I hoped so.* Knowing Sarah, she probably had it memorized.

I took one last look both ways down the corridor. Nothing. Not a soul.

"Here goes nothing." I held my breath.

I pushed the door that used to open to Sarah's room.

Lightning flashed outside the window on the far stone wall, revealing a long, curved room littered with debris. Heavy, dark curtains draped down from the ceiling.

I got the feeling that something alive was hiding in the dark. I could practically hear it breathing. I could almost feel its stare.

I stepped forward carefully, not quite committed to going in. "Sarah?" I called to the darkness, holding my candle *far* in front.

A soft whimpering floated inside the room, to the left. It sounded like a girl crying in the darkness, so faint I could barely hear it over the rain outside.

The darkness beyond the candle swam in inky circles, no matter how hard I tried to stare through it.

I swallowed hard and stepped into the room, carefully watching the floor for loose stones or pieces of rotted wood. Falling with a lit candle would be a very bad idea.

Carefully, I moved toward the sound.

On the floor, the candle glow revealed the well-rounded ends of broken table legs, shattered drawers from splintered dressers, a black, shiny case with a large knife and a small knife, each encrusted with glittering stones, and . . . the edge of a bed.

The bed was very tall, with small wooden steps leading up to the mattress. The posts on the corners spiraled up to a gold cloth canopy, splotched white and green and rotting in several places. It seemed too narrow, slimmer than my bed and real short.

As I passed the foot board, I nearly fell over a low chest covered with rotted, wooden sandals, each with rusted metal clasps and cracked, leather straps.

A mob of insects scurried from under the candlelight, disappearing into the cracks and hollows of the chest.

It looked like a girl's room *would* have looked in a castle, I supposed.

The whimpering! I heard it again.

I froze, afraid to move a muscle.

It was coming from the other side of the bed, close to the floor and against the wall.

My eyes grew wide with shock as the candle glow revealed Sarah, curled tight in a terrified ball between the bed and the wall.

Her hair hung down, soaking wet. Her eyes were fixed and staring, her whole body trembling. Her mouth gaped open and closed, trying to form a word.

She looked as if she had seen a . . .

She pointed behind me.

I turned and saw the mirror as lightning flashed outside, revealing its full, ghastly form.

About five feet high, it had been shoved into a corner and propped against the wall.

Curling ivy crept up the sides, carved deep into the oval, wooden frame. The mirror surface, cracked and covered in dust, reflected almost the entire bedroom, including a portrait I hadn't noticed before.

I looked over to the far wall, near the door, where the portrait *should* have been hanging.

There was nothing there. Just blank wall.

I looked back. The portrait was *still* in the

mirror. *Impossible!* It was reflected in the mirror, but it wasn't on the wall.

"Sarah. What is it? What did you see?" I whispered, unable to contain the trembling in my voice. *Something* had scared her, something about the mirror.

She didn't respond. Only pointed. To the portrait in the mirror.

The portrait became clearer.

It showed a young woman in a weird, puffy hat, with a scarf tied under her chin. Her eyes drooped with terrible sadness.

Suddenly, I *felt* someone coming, like someone walking toward us from the dark. The hair on the back of my neck stood up. I could hear the steady shuffling, or was it just my imagination?

I rose slowly and started toward the mirror, the dreadful sensation growing.

"Simon, no. You don't understand. Don't go near it," Sarah sobbed.

I placed the candle down at my feet and swallowed hard. I reached out, determined to touch the mirror's surface.

"NOOOOO! She's in there!" Sarah cried, scooting back against the wall, curling into an even tighter ball.

As my fingers touched the surface of the mirror. . .

a woman appeared behind me, her image reflected in the glass!

The woman from the portrait!

Her eyes were fixed and staring, her head cocked to the side. Her hands covered her mouth as trickles of blood ran down her chin.

I screamed and spun around.

Nothing! Only Sarah, hiding her eyes, balled in the corner.

I turned back to the mirror.

The lady stood right in front of me, in front of the mirror!

Her icy hands grabbed my shoulders, and she fixed me with a freezing stare. Her mouth, flecked with blood, opened and closed, but only a raspy gurgle emerged.

"For ... forrrr ... givvve," she rasped, clawing at my arms, trying to pull me closer, as the candle blew out at my feet.

I pulled away and ran.

In a lightning flash, I saw Sarah scramble across the bed. It fell with a CRASH as she raced for the door.

Neither of us looked back.

Together we cried out and ran into the safety of the hallway, pulling the door shut behind us.

"DID YOU SEE THAT?" I gasped.

"I saw her in the mirror before you got here. E-Every time I moved, s-she appeared," Sarah stammered.

We both held the door shut.

I struggled to catch my breath. "Well, at least we're out of there. Safe for the moment."

Then I noticed the figure down the hall, staring at us.

We were not alone.

12

Another female figure stood silently at the top of the stairs, just down the hall.

A candle flickered in one hand, lighting her side with an eerie, yellow glow. In the other hand she held a large wicker basket. A large bonnet drooped down over her face, concealing her features.

"Great. *Another* creepy lady," I said, swallowing hard.

The woman started walking down the hall toward us, the basket bouncing on her swaying arm.

Sarah didn't say anything. She simply stared at the approaching figure, her face dotted with cold sweat.

We stood frozen in terror, still standing in front of the closed door to Sarah's room.

Sarah choked, "Simon. Can you move?"

"No, I really can't." I replied. My mind screamed to run. My legs tried, but I couldn't move. *I stood frozen in horror.*

Sarah continued, "I think I know w-w-where we are."

The woman came closer, steadily approaching, never looking up.

"Haunted castle?"

"Yep."

Let me guess, you saw it on the D-Discovery C-Channel, right?" I stammered.

"I think so."

"Which castle?" I asked, watching the basket sway on the woman's arm.

"I'm not sure. I'm trying to remember," Sarah replied, close to tears, as the woman came up to us and paused.

Her hooded head turned and looked at us both slowly, cautiously. We couldn't see her face. Her plain, brown dress hung off her body like a sack.

In a quiet, muffled voice, the woman asked, "Would you help me with my basket?"

We nodded blankly in unison. What could we say? She stretched her arm toward me and handed me the heavy wicker basket. With a slack jaw . . . I took it. *I felt compelled to take it, like I didn't have a choice.*

She continued down the hall and we followed, though I don't know why. It was like we were under a spell. I carried the basket in one hand, and wiped the sweat from my face with the other. Sarah walked right beside me, clutching my arm tightly. "Excuse me, lady. But could you tell us where we are exactly? This used to be our house, and I was just wondering . . ."

The woman giggled softly, teasingly, muffled inside her big bonnet.

Sarah continued, "Could you tell us who the owner of the castle is? The Baron? . . ."

The woman giggled some more, almost laughing. "Is the basket too heavy for you?"

"No," I replied, shifting the basket to my right hand, next to Sarah. It was heavy and covered with a cloth.

The woman giggled again, a muffled, mocking laugh.

Sarah looked down at the basket, a look of growing horror spreading across her pale face.

She stared up at the figure walking in front of us, fear making her voice crack. "Uh, would you mind me asking . . . w-where are you going?"

"The tower. By order of the Baron," the woman cackled, laughing insanely.

"SIMON! NO!" Sarah screamed, knocking the basket from my hands.

The basket hit the floor and something white rolled out; white as a sheet with long, flowing hair, glistening teeth and dark eyes.

Her head!

Her head was in the basket!

We both screamed as the figure turned, its bonnet dropping back, revealing empty shoulders with outstretched hands!

We ran past her, sprinting down the hall as fast as we could fly.

I looked over my shoulder and saw her running behind us, holding the head up like a lantern, swinging it back and forth, laughing with a ghostly echo.

With a sudden toss, the head flew from her hand, past our running feet, to land in the hallway in front of us.

"TONIGHT'S THE NIGHT!" The head screeched, its bone-white teeth chattering, its eyes staring blankly, its white hair spreading in tangles on the floor.

I kicked it *hard* as we ran past, stark horror pulsing through my body, pushing my legs like pile drivers.

"QUICK! IN THERE!" Sarah screamed, pointing to an open doorway at the corner of the upstairs hall.

Without thinking, I followed her inside. The door closed behind us with a slam.

We gasped for breath, our hearts pounding, our minds racing. I felt wave after wave of nausea pound my stomach as I thought about the head, *lying in the hall.*

"Where . . . Where are we?" I asked.

Torches blazed to life on the wall and suddenly . . . *I wished I hadn't asked.*

"Oh, great! Go in there, you said! Now look where you p-p-put us!" I stammered, stepping over a skeleton, walking toward the middle of the room.

Skeletons. I found it hard to take my eyes off them. I felt sick just looking at them. I fought back wave after wave of panic.

Torches blazed on the walls, revealing the room's ghastly contents. We seemed to be in a tower chamber; a very plain room with a high ceiling, windowless walls and a floor littered with skeletons. Dozens of them. It smelled like the air in the room had been sealed there for centuries. Some of the walls looked as if they had been raked with claws.

"I panicked, okay? I thought I heard the voice coming from the basket, and when she said she was going to the tower, I *knew* what was in that basket," Sarah said, trembling and clutching herself tightly.

"What do you mean?"

"Towers were sometimes used as prisons, torture chambers, or . . . execution halls. You know, the chopping block? That lady must have committed some crime against the lord of the castle," Sarah said, fear creeping into her voice.

"So where are we now?" I asked.

"I don't know. There are so many haunted castles, I have no idea which one this is. It could be German, Scottish, English . . . take your pick. Maybe if I saw it from the outside, or maybe some more of the living areas . . ."

I bent carefully, examining a skeleton. Despite the sickening horror swelling in my throat, I thought maybe I could find some clue to help. It seemed to be clothed in rags, covered in cobwebs and the bones looked all scratched . . . or *chewed*.

"So, who do you think *these* guys are?" I asked, dropping a bony arm back to the floor in a cloud of dust.

"I don't know. It's a whole family, that's for sure. Look at how many different sizes of skeletons there are."

She was right. Little skeletons and big skeletons covered the floor, stacked on top of each other. Shreds of clothing still remained on some. The smaller ones had plain dresses, while the larger ones wore baggy shirts. I even saw little kid skeletons.

"I hope *we* won't be joining them . . . THE DOOR!" I cried.

It was gone.

A solid stone wall stood where the door used to be! My hands clawed at the stones, searching for an opening, a crack, anything!

"It's not here! The door is gone," I sobbed. Then my eyes fell back to the skeletons on the floor.

"Maybe that's how they died. They were trapped in here! Walled in, with no way out! They must have starved!" Sarah cried.

"Who would . . . that rotten, little ghost! This is all *his* fault. Who is he? Why is he doing this? Why did he turn our house into a haunted castle?" I asked, my anger swelling by the second.

"I don't know, but I do know we have to get out of here!" Sarah cried, panic pushing her around the walls, desperately searching for a way out.

Suddenly the torches flickered and went out. An inky blackness smothered the room like a blanket.

"Sarah? Are you okay?" I called from the center of the room, afraid to move, fearing I'd fall onto a skeleton.

I had the feeling again, like someone was approaching. The unmistakable feeling of someone else being in the room swept over me.

"What's going on?" Sarah gasped as she ran toward the center of the room, hoping I was still there.

A pale, blue glow drifted up from the floor, from underneath the skeletons. The thin mist rose ankle deep from the floor.

With horror, I watched as *people* rose from the mist. Shadowy, ghostly outlines of *people!*

They rose from the skeletons and ran up to the walls, pounding, clawing, screaming in desperation. Their ghostly hands passing through claw marks made long ago.

Their hideous shrieks pierced my ears, filling me with dread as I realized . . .

We were trapped with them.

All around us, they screamed and cried, holding each other. Some clutched ghostly babies tightly. Others cursed at the walls, as if someone on the other side could hear. All glowed a pale, transparent blue.

"It's gotta be the ghosts of the people who died in here! The skeletons!" I yelled over the commotion.

"An entire family!" Sarah screamed out, sobbing and clutching at my arm.

Suddenly they faded away, vanishing into the darkness.

Silence.

"T-They're gone."

"No, wait. LOOK!" Sarah cried, pointing all around.

They slowly *returned,* fading back into light, but now seemingly uninterested in the walls. They turned to us, their sorrowful eyes piercing us with haunting stares.

Like a pack of animals, they suddenly attacked.

They *surrounded* us, begging us for freedom, clawing at us, screaming, "WHY?"

Dozens of icy cold, transparent hands gripped my arms, my legs. Their tortured, leering faces completely surrounded me.

"Go away!" I screamed, knocking them away as fast as I could.

"Leave us alone! LEAVE US ALONE!" Sarah cried, slumping to the floor.

A section of the wall across from the door collapsed! A secret passage was revealed behind it. Our only hope.

"SARAH! Come on!" I cried.

We burst through the crowd and ran to the ragged hole in the wall, the ghosts' sickening howls of pain following close behind.

As we dodged into the hidden passageway, I noticed that the ghostly, pitiful mob *stopped*. As we fled, they merely watched unmoving, sinking back into the floor.

I paused at the hole, amazed.

One by one, the ghosts vanished, until only a single mother was left clutching her crying, ghostly baby. She rocked slowly, her back against the wall near the door.

Her gaze filled my heart with the deepest sorrow I have ever felt. She muttered, "Tonight's the night," then vanished . . .

I trembled, my legs nearly giving out beneath me. My pulse quickened at the mention of that phrase.

"*What* happens tonight?" I found myself whispering.

Sarah grabbed my shoulder, "COME ON! HURRY!"

Little did I realize, an unbelievable terror awaited us . . .

just down the hall.

14

The passageway curved and twisted ahead of us, with an occasional torch lighting dim circles on the ruined, stone floor.

Curtains of cobwebs covered our faces as we ran forward, stumbling over broken arches and rotted, wooden timbers.

We slowed to a crawl as the rubble in the hallway grew more dense. My sides ached and my head throbbed. I noticed deep gashes and cuts in the wooden beams lining the walls, as if a wild animal had chewed its way through the hall.

"Where do you think this leads? Do you have any idea where we are? Anything look familiar?" I asked breathlessly, hoping she would remember anything from that stupid show she taped off the Discovery Channel. Anything to help us.

"I don't know. It looks like some kind of secret passage. Sometimes castles had secret passages, so the garrison could get from tower to tower without being seen."

"Garrison?" I asked. I could see Sarah struggling to remember everything she could about castles, but the fear made it difficult.

"The garrison were the castle guards. They protected the castle from invaders and helped the lord of the castle control the land he ruled," Sarah replied, her voice cracking.

"Did they ever wear armor?"

"Yeah, sometimes, why?"

"LOOK!" I yelled, pointing ahead.

A suit of armor lay face down in the middle of the passageway, made of tiny, linked chains and metal plates. Light from a torch on the wall glinted off its back. Stones from the ceiling had fallen and crushed the legs, pinning it solidly to the floor.

A small, narrow doorway stood at the end of the passage, just a few yards beyond the armor. We couldn't go back. No way we were going to risk that chamber of skeletons again.

"W-we have to get to that door. Stay close and don't touch the armor," I choked, my back to the wall, moving forward carefully with a cautious sidestep.

Neither of us took our eyes off the still figure as we shuffled past, holding our breaths. "Just a little bit more," I whispered.

My whisper turned into a scream.

Sarah's eyes grew wide in disbelief. The armor stirred, and began to rise. It bent at the waist at an impossible angle, its legs still pinned to the floor!

My mind flew into a frenzy as I watched the baggy, cloth arms reach up to its battered helmet. With gloved hands, it flipped the visor up, revealing a mashed, skull face and hideous, glowing red eyes. It screamed at us both, as if in terrible pain!

I felt my heart quicken, threatening to burst. My face flushed in panic as it reached for me, waving its arms crazily. I froze in absolute terror as it grabbed my leg.

IT HAD ME! IT HAD ME!

A freezing cold sensation swept my spine.

Sarah pulled me away with a shriek and we flew through the door at the end of passageway, slamming it shut behind us.

15

I choked back tears, trying to brush the image from my mind. It felt like death itself had touched me. The echoes of the chilling touch clawed my spine as Sarah tried to calm me down.

"Simon! Simon! You're okay now! You're all right! It couldn't get out from under the rubble! It can't come after us . . ."

Slowly, the chilling feeling passed and my mind began to clear. The effects of that thing's touch began to wear off. It almost felt like a spell.

"I could feel it, Sarah. I could feel its panic, its f-fright . . . its p-pain! It's like it passed along what it f-felt," I gasped, trying to focus on her face. "I-I'm all right. I-It's okay. W-Where are we n-now?"

"We're in another tower, I think," Sarah

said, gazing about.

It looked like the other tower room, the one with the skeletons. Large, round, no windows. The only door was the one we came through, but across the room, I saw *a trapdoor*. The wooden hatch lay open, leaving a large, square hole in the floor.

"No way I'm going in there," I muttered.

Then I noticed the bed, a simple, iron cot with a mattress made of straw. Beside it, set flush against the wall, sat a rotted desk with a broken chair. "This must have been *someone's* room."

Sarah approached the desk first.

"Yeah, but whose? Look at this!" she exclaimed, picking up a chain with a wide, iron hoop on the end.

"What is it?" I asked.

"It's a manacle," she muttered, puzzled by the sight. She pulled at the chain, bolted into the floor beside the desk. "It's like a dog leash. They used it on prisoners, to keep them from going anywhere."

"So, this is a prison cell?" I asked, pushing down on the desktop, testing its sturdiness. It creaked and groaned as I pressed. No way I was going to try the chair.

"No. This is some kind of a secret room.

Prison towers weren't built like this. It's too small. This room was built to hide something . . . or someone for a long, long time. See? They had a bed, a desk and a chair. But why would they need a manacle?"

"Maybe they had a pet."

"Maybe . . . or. . . Wait a minute. What's that?" Sarah suddenly crouched on the floor and reached under the desk.

"What are you doing? Are you nuts? There could be spiders, or snakes or who knows what . . .," I cried out, grabbing her shoulder. She pulled something out . . .

"Blocks?" I asked. *Children's blocks.* Letters, numbers and pictures decorated their sides, painted in drab colors.

She continued to reach under the desk, pulling out old, yellowed papers with large scrawls, alphabets, terrible drawings. They looked like a child's drawings.

"What is all this? A kid lived here? All locked up? Hidden away from the rest of the castle?" It didn't make sense.

Suddenly Sarah's face flushed, then grew pale, dotted with sweat. She stood bolt upright as if lightning had struck her.

"I remember this story from the television show I saw," she said gravely, swallowing hard.

"It's not a nice story, is it? I don't want to know who lives in here, do I?" I choked, backing away from the desk.

She turned to face me and froze.

"Si-Si-Simon, be-be-behind you," Sarah could hardly squeak above a whisper. Her eyes locked onto the wall behind me as her face drained to ghostly white.

I turned slowly and saw a shadow spread across the wall, cast by something coming up . . . *through the trapdoor.*

Sarah and I clung together, peering anxiously as we saw *it* emerge.

A huge, misshapen head poked up out of the trapdoor. Two large eyes peered out from beneath a mound of wispy, black hair. It shifted its terrible eyes from side to side, and then looked squarely at *us.*

A giggle escaped its twisted, puckering mouth as it crawled out, huge hands dragging its crumpled body across the floor.

It took obvious glee as it stalked us, circling to the side against the wall, its mouth open in an idiot's smile. Its childlike, gurgling laugh sent shivers down my spine.

Sarah and I backed away as it circled around toward the desk, never taking its eyes off us. We backed toward the trapdoor, *where it came from.*

I hated the way it moved. It would move very, very slowly, using its hands to drag itself ... and then it would RUSH AHEAD, its laugh keeping its pace; its shriveled, tiny legs flopping uselessly behind.

It stared at the blocks lying on the floor, and then suddenly *charged* for us, furious, its palms slapping the stone floor as fast as footsteps.

"THE TRAPDOOR! GO! GO! GOOO!" I yelled, panic speeding my legs.

We ran to the trapdoor and saw a narrow stone staircase spiraling down into darkness.

For a brief moment we paused, the darkness below making us reconsider.

"Simon?" Sarah whimpered, as if begging not to go any further.

Then a loud, wailing cry from behind sent us rushing down, down, down the spiral staircase ...

and into the biggest surprise of all.

16

Our hands felt along the slimy stone walls as we worked our way down the darkened staircase.

"Be careful, Sarah," I called from the darkness. "These stairs are narrow and slippery. I-I don't think it's following us."

"Yeah, right," her voice echoed from the gloom, waaaay on down the stairs, far ahead of me.

"Hey! Wait for me."

Sarah reached the bottom long before I did.

I saw her push through a dark, heavy cloth hung over an opening in the wall at the bottom of the stairs. *Light* flickered into the passage from behind the cloth.

"All right! Light!" I cheered, pushing through the cloth after Sarah. "Oh, man. NO WAY!" I cried in astonishment.

At the bottom of the stairs was a room.

The walls of the room towered over us, at least fifty feet high, each wall lined with rows and rows of books. Large wooden tables lined with rickety wooden chairs sat in front of the largest fireplace I had ever seen, a huge fire roaring inside.

Iron candle holders filled with candles sat on each table, covered in cobwebs.

"A library!" I cried, stumbling forward. The cloth tapestry fell back against the wall, covering the secret passageway behind me, hiding it well. "What do you . . ."

Sarah had already climbed a thin ladder leaning against a bookshelf. Her eyes scanned the titles on the spines of the enormous volumes. She didn't waste *any* time.

"At least now maybe we'll get some answers," I said.

I felt a little relieved. If anyone could find a way out of this mess in those books, Sarah could. She's a total research hound! Still, there had to be thousands of books lining the shelves. THOUSANDS! And only *two* of us.

"Well? What do you think? Can you find something to get rid of that rotten, lousy, glowing, blue booger and turn our house back to normal?"

Sarah picked a volume off the shelf and opened the cover, dust falling out in sheets. "I don't know . . . This could take a while."

"What exactly are you looking for?"

"Something on the history of this castle. The people who lived here. We have to find out who the little ghost *is*. We need to find out why he was in that trunk in the first place."

"I don't get it," I plopped down at a table near the fire. It felt great! The warmth brought some of my courage back.

Sarah came over and set a stack of books down in front of me.

"From what I remember, ghosts haunt places where they died, or places where they left something undone. He was in the trunk for a reason, I'm sure. We have to find out why. Then maybe we'll figure out how to get rid of him," she mumbled, more to herself than me.

As she shuffled away to get more books, I flipped through the first pages of the one in front of me. Ugh. It read like Greek.

"This *could* take awhile," I groaned.

On and on, I read and read. Nothing. Page after page of family trees, castle records and battle histories. My eyes blurred and strained under the flickering light of the candles on the table. The candles were tall when I started. Now they were nearly gone.

"I can't find anything! Absolutely nothing helpful!" I yelled to Sarah, who was moving from shelf to shelf systematically, searching for anything that might help.

"Just keep reading, Simon. We have to find something!" Sarah yelled back.

I found myself wishing for a pencil. A marker. A pen. Anything to doodle with. The itch to draw on the borders of the books gnawed at me. What a great Kyle Banner cartoon *this* place would make. It would be the ultimate to see *him* trapped in a haunted castle. A ghostly COOL DOG YAK, grabbing him from the dark. Yeah. Cool.

Another pile of books plopped down in front of me, nearly knocking my candle rack over. "HEY! Watch it! You nearly . . ."

The words caught in my throat.

A young girl stood on the other side of the table, staring at me sadly, glowing a brilliant white. *She* had dropped the books in front of me. She was dressed in a long, white gown with a long sash.

"S-S-Sarah . . . SARAH! LOOK QUICK!" I yelled, jumping up and away from the table.

The girl turned and floated toward a wide doorway on the far end of the library. The huge wooden doors opened for her as she approached them, then closed silently behind her after she passed through.

"D-D-Did you see that?" I cried, pointing to the ghostly mist still swirling in the air near the door.

"See what? What's wrong with you? Hey, HEY! Where did you get THOSE BOOKS! That's what we need!" Sarah's eyes lit as bright as the fireplace.

"But . . . But . . . the girl . . . oh, never mind." I stopped even trying to explain. Sarah had already dug into one of the books. She barely knew I was in the room.

"It's the recent history of the castle. The last tenants. And LOOK! There's the lord of the castle and . . . Oh, no."

Oh, no was right.

17

It was like a rogue's gallery of everyone we had run into so far. We saw unwelcome but very familiar faces on page after page.

"It's the entire history of the family of the castle! . . . And about the horrible lord of the castle! The Baron! It's exactly what we were looking for!" Sarah cried excitedly.

"Cool! Read on, Einstein! Find out who that little blue ghost is and get us out of this mess!" I felt my excitement grow as well.

"Hmmm. Look. It's the woman in the mirror with the bloody mouth," Sarah said, pointing at the book.

I stared at the portrait. The exact same painting that revealed itself in the mirror in Sarah's old room. "Yeah, that's her. Sad eyes and all. Terrible grip."

"The Baron's mother. It says here, he had her tongue removed for yelling at him at a party, or some kind of reception."

"That's pretty drastic," I nodded.

"Here, it talks about a whole noble family who fled from a neighboring castle when it was attacked. They came here for shelter. The Baron invited them in, put them in a tower to hide them and . . . trapped them there, letting them starve."

"Not a very good neighbor," I mumbled. "OH, WAIT! The skeletons! All those ghosts who attacked us in that room with no doors, trying to get out of the tower! It was them!"

"Ewwww. Recognize her?" Sarah pointed at another drawing.

"Oh, yeah. She looks a lot different . . . with her head."

"Simon, that's gross. She was the sister of the Baron. He had her head cut off because she didn't approve of his choice . . . for a wife."

"Wife? Who would marry this guy?"

"I don't know, but look here."

I looked at an illustration of about twenty guys in chain-mail armor, all standing in front of a burning village.

"I'll bet the knight who grabbed you in the hall was one of these guys, the garrison of the castle. It says they were terrible. Little more than hired thugs, doing the Baron's dirty work."

"Wait. What's that around that guy's neck?" I asked, pointing to the guard on the end, holding a sword.

"It's an iron star. People used iron symbols in those days to ward off evil spirits. They hung iron faces or horseshoes over their doors to keep the evil ghosts out," Sarah explained, turning the page.

"I wonder if it worked . . . Hey, what about Ugly? You know. The thing in the kid's room with the blocks?" Just thinking about it slithering across the floor made me sick to my stomach.

Sarah flipped page after page, looking puzzled. "I don't know. All it says is that there were rumors of a hidden brother, a hideous monster, kept chained in a secret room in the castle. No one could talk about him without fear of imprisonment. It was also rumored that secret passages were built to allow the brother to move about the castle unseen. He died alone . . . by his brother's hand." Sarah swallowed hard.

"The Baron."

Sarah nodded.

"Boy, oh boy. I do NOT want to meet this Baron guy." I sighed, a cold chill sweeping through the room.

"Simon, we already have. LOOK!"

I couldn't believe it.

According to the painting in the book, he stood about four feet tall. His head was squat and wide, his eyes bugged and staring. Long, bony arms grew from a shrimpy, little body. A puckering mouth perched on his twisted, pale face. What a noble portrait. No mistaking it. No doubt in my mind. The only difference . . . in the painting, he was *alive.*

It was the little blue ghost from the trunk who wrecked our kitchen, swallowed the babysitter, changed our house into a haunted castle and plastered my cartoons all over Kyle Banner's walls.

The little blue ghost was the Baron, the lord of the castle . . .

"Oscar Bluecher," Sarah said.

"Only a name that *hideous* could fit a rotten, lousy, glowing blue booger like that!" I yelled. "What a rat! What a creep! What's his story? How do we stop him?"

Sarah read a bit further . . .
and then told me.
I threw an absolute fit.
"WHAT!? WE HAVE TO DO WHAT? You gotta be kidding me! Say that again?"

"We have to get him back in the trunk," Sarah said again.

"WHAT? You can't be serious! How do you propose we do that? Oh, I get it! You nail a little diving board to the side, and I'll hang a sign that says, GHOST POOL! DIVE RIGHT IN!"

"Getting upset isn't going to help anything, Simon. We have to get him back in the trunk."

"Why?" I asked, trying to calm down.

Sarah continued talking, unruffled. She was in major 'teacher' mode.

"It's pretty terrible. What happened to him, I mean. I know he did a lot of horrible things to people but listen to this . . .

"*On his wedding day, despite the strong*

protests of his mother and his sister, he locked his bride away, in the tower prison . . . to keep her from running away.

"That afternoon, he had all the bodies of his enemies (like the family he trapped and starved) placed around the wedding hall in the chapel, like decorations. To show his bride that she had better never give him any trouble, like running away.

"You already know that his mother and sister didn't attend," Sarah said, looking up at me from the pages of the book.

"Wait! Why? Because . . . oh, yeah. The tongue and head thing. Okay. Sorry. Go on."

"Anyway. He had to drag his wife-to-be, kicking and screaming, down the aisle of the chapel, the garrison standing guard at all the exits to make sure she couldn't get away. All the guests were amazed at his shocking display of cruelty.

"When the minister finally told him to kiss the bride, she refused, crying "NO"!

"She kicked him and ran, all the way up to the top of the high balcony that overlooked the chapel.

"Furious, he chased her and grabbed her,

struggling on the balcony in front of all the
wedding guests.

"With a horrid shriek, they both fell onto
the marble floor below.

"They buried her in the courtyard that
same day, still in her wedding dress.

"The guests and the garrison, full of
hatred and disgust for the Baron, shoved him in
a trunk and hid him in the castle."

"Wow. That's pretty gruesome. Where'd
they hide the trunk?"

Sarah closed the book slowly and gulped.

"In the library."

After a few minutes of poking around,
peering behind tapestries and moving dozens of
books, Sarah and I found ourselves kneeling
beside the trunk . . . again.

We found it hidden in a small niche, behind
a covering stone, right beside the fireplace.

"Here we go again," I huffed, flipping the
latches up, one by one.

All but the central latch.

Sarah and I looked at each other.

"You want to do the honors?" I asked,
nervously.

Sarah stared at the trunk and thought a moment. She looked at me with an expression of grim determination.

"Yeah. I'll do it this time."

Sarah grabbed the central latch and FLIPPED IT UP!

We jumped back as the trunk lid flew open, expecting the same explosion.

Nothing. Only a plume of dust and a horrid, rotting smell.

"Oh, man. It's worse than before. Like the bottom of your closet times ten."

Sarah elbowed me in the ribs as we leaned over to peer in.

The web-covered, mummified skeleton of Baron Oscar Bluecher sat folded inside, still in his wedding robe. A spider scurried across his face, disappearing into the darkness of the trunk.

"It's him," we said gravely, in unison.

I saw a dim, blue spark crackle in his hollow, web-lined eye sockets.

"Wait a minute, what was that?" I shouted, bolting to my feet. "Did you see that?"

Sarah looked up at me from the floor, a look of puzzlement on her face. "See what?"

With a terrible shriek, the mummified

skeleton jerked up out of the trunk and grabbed Sarah around the neck! Eyes grew back in the sockets, swelling like balloons. Its withered arms blistered and puffed, as did the rest of its body. Blue, smoky light surrounded it, coursing across the grey skin.

The ghost had found its body, and brought it back to life, like a ghastly puppet. He was waiting for us to find his body!

"NOOOOO!" I cried as the hideous little skeleton jumped out of the trunk and ran toward the doors at the end of the library, dragging Sarah along, kicking and screaming!

"Simon! Help me! SIMON! NOOO!" Sarah cried.

"**TONIGHT'S THE NIGHT!**" it screamed and cackled.

"SARAH!" I yelled, too petrified to move, terrified beyond words.

I watched the doors close behind them.

A growing horror and dread jolted my legs, making me weak and light-headed.

"The *wedding* is tonight. *That's* what he's talking about. That's what they were *ALL* talking about. The wedding . . . and this time, *Sarah's the bride.*"

19

I ran to the library doors and threw them open, rushing through, desperate to stop the evil Baron, Oscar Bluecher, from marrying my sister.

A long hallway with tall stone arches stretched in front of me, half the length of a football field at least. A single red carpet, trimmed in gold, ran the length of the hall.

Rain pounded against the stained-glass windows set between the arches. Pale, blue light from the nighttime sky filtered through, revealing large, bowl-shaped stone planters, grown over with large vines. They sat under each window, about a dozen of them.

"SIMON! HELP ME! QUICK! HE'S C-C-CHOKING ME!" I heard a voice call from the end of the hall. "LET ME GOOOO!"

Sarah.

With horror, I watched the terrible little skeleton drag Sarah up a short set of stairs, to a large arched doorway at the end of the hall.

"WAIT!" I yelled, running even though I knew it was too late.

The door closed behind them and I noticed a small ghostly boy dressed in rags, sitting on the lowest step, staring at me.

"Here," a sweet voice called from behind, stopping me. Suddenly, I felt something slide over my neck, and something heavy thud against my chest.

It was an amulet, shaped like a horseshoe . . . on a cord.

"An iron horseshoe?" I gasped in surprise.

I turned and saw the girl, the same glowing girl in white who had given me the books. She was beautiful, with flowing red hair and very sad eyes. Her dress flowed far behind her, fanning out on the red carpet.

"It will protect you from evil spirits," she whispered, then faded away.

"Sarah. I have to get to Sarah." I turned and continued to run down the hall, the boy staring at me from the steps, *giggling.*

Suddenly, as if signalled by the boy's

laugh, the vines began to grow. They spread out of the planters, snaking across the floor, tangling upon themselves . . . *across my feet.*

I cried out and stumbled, tripping over the rope-like tangles. Rolling end over end down the hall, until I could see nothing but rotted green leaves, and feel nothing but scratching, clawing vines.

They snaked around my arms, my legs.

I felt them crawl up my pants and my shirt. Across my eyes, blindfolding me.

Wrapping tight around my throat.

I pulled and tugged with all my might but couldn't break their grasp.

I tried to scream, but couldn't. The moldy leaves gagged my mouth.

They pulled tighter and tighter, until I could barely breathe.

I couldn't move, no matter how hard I struggled. My fists clenched, and my legs kicked, but it didn't help. The vines had an unnatural strength.

Then I heard footsteps crunching down the hall, across the vines . . . *toward me.*

I heard two voices, low and grumbling.

"Is this the one? The one going to the

tower?" a voice growled.

"That's the one. It's the block for him, The brother of the bride," another voice replied.

I struggled harder, panicked, my heart pounding. The block, they said. They were going to chop off my head! Just like the Baron's sister. Sarah was doomed, same as me, if I couldn't break free.

I felt cold, steel gloves grab my shirt and yank me up, pulling me free of the tangled, terrible vines.

I clawed away the leaves from my face, my eyes . . . *and screamed.*

A large, armor-suited *skeleton* held me by the shirt, another right beside him. Their eyes glowed fierce red and they peered at me with a burning hate.

"LET ME DOWN!" I yelled as they laughed.

"We'll let you down, ONTO THE CHOPPING BLOCK MY YOUNG FRIEND! And then..."

Suddenly, the ghostly guard shrieked and dropped me, the sight of the iron horseshoe around my neck sending it reeling back in horror.

"Wow. This thing really works!" I said

with growing astonishment, as the guards backed slowly away.

"Go on, GET OUT OF HERE! GET! growled, holding my horseshoe in front of me, thrusting it toward them with each step.

They ran past me, trampling the vines, scrambling into the library as fast as they could go.

"All right, ghost-boy! Get out of the way!" I growled, stomping through the dead vines covering the floor, marching up the steps to the door.

The servant boy looked at me with shock and surprise and cried, almost pleading . . .

"*I'm so sorry, sir. I-I sneaked out of the wedding. I'm very sorry, sir. Please. You won't tell, will you? He'll do terrible things to me, sir. You don't understand. He'll . . .*"

The boy screamed and vanished, the sound of a whip cracking in the air fading with him.

My hand pressed against the door.

I clutched my horseshoe, hoping it still worked, and pushed through the door into the . . . *wedding chapel.*

The archway door opened into the largest chapel I could have imagined. My eyes nearly fell from my head trying to take it all in. The feeling of death and sadness surrounded me.

"Whoa. I had no idea," I gasped, stunned by the sights and the sounds.

The ceiling seemed miles overhead, domed and covered with cracked tiles and rotted wooden beams. A high balcony overlooked the room, jutting from the far wall over a small alcove.

Dozens of skeletons hung from the ceiling beams, their lower jaws dropped in silly grins. All different shapes and sizes. *Hung like decorations.*

A ghostly organ filled the cathedral with eerie music.

Dead flowers drooped in every corner.

My eyes drifted down to the hundreds of hideous, ghostly guests lining the benches and waiting in the aisles.

Some looked vaguely familiar, others didn't.

I saw a large, bearded man fiddling with a deck of cards, coughing loudly and clearing his throat.

Beside him slouched a man in a long, black overcoat, his face hidden behind a tall, floppy collar.

Pale ladies in ghostly grey wept silently, hanging their heads and swaying back and forth, clutching at handkerchiefs.

One skull-faced young man seemed hardly able to contain himself. He rocked back and forth, in and out of the aisle, as if dying to run a race. His skeletal hands twisted themselves into knots.

I noticed a woman's hand raise up in the crowd, holding a ghostly head up like a lantern. I supposed it was to see better.

Then I saw the twisted, misshapen brother from the kid's room, squirming into the aisle, dragging his hands, waddling back and forth, and laughing with excitement.

With a gasp, I closed the door quietly and slipped to the side. No one seemed to notice me. *So far so good.*

Now if I could only find . . .

Then I saw Sarah.

She kicked and clawed and struggled with the evil Baron, Oscar Bluecher, at the end of the aisle, in front of a rotted, wooden altar. A fat, bearded ghost in a white robe was reading from a book in front of them. *A minister.*

I couldn't understand what he was saying, but I didn't really have to. I knew what he was doing. *He was marrying them.*

Sarah's screams and cries echoed down the aisle. The evil Baron held her tightly, yelling for the minister to read faster.

"Oh, no. Oh, man," I mumbled to myself. I did *NOT* want to go down that center aisle. There were too many of them! They would all try and stop me. How could I hope to live through it? Every part of me wanted to sneak down the sides, figure out some way to stop it quietly, without attracting too much attention.

But deep down, I knew there was no time.

"And I thought a fight with Kyle Banner would be bad." I held the horseshoe tightly, stepped forward into the aisle and yelled, "STOP THE WEDDING!"

Hundreds of ghostly heads turned in my direction.

21

I ran down the center aisle, as fast as I could go, the ghosts closing in on me.

They scrambled over the benches and slithered across seats, rushing me from all sides. Their cries and moans chilled my blood, as they clawed and clutched at me.

Their hands and faces pulled away in gasping horror as I held my iron horseshoe up for protection, plunging through the gathering crowd.

Suddenly, the ghastly mother with her bloody mouth grabbed my shoulders, like in Sarah's room before. Her eyes glowed; her mouth dripped a steady, red stream.

"LET GO OF ME!" I screamed, pulling away and ducking past.

A woman's head flopped onto the floor in

front of me. *The sister!*

"Stop him! Stop him! He must not interfere!" her head screamed crazily, her teeth clacking, her eyes blazing.

Once again, I kicked her head *hard* as I ran past.

Above me, the poor skeletons hanging from the beams screamed and cried, calling down to me, "Let...it...end! Do not interfere! Let...it...end!"

I ignored them, rapidly approaching the end of the aisle. I could see Sarah still struggling against the Baron, and the minister still reading from the book.

Two ghostly guards stepped in front of me, large gleaming swords in their hands. Their visors raised up, revealing cracked skull faces and glowing red eyes.

"YOU'RE OURS NOW!" they cried.

I ducked under their swinging swords.

They hit each other with a loud CLANK, knocking themselves into the benches on both sides. "SARAH!" I screamed.

The minister read quickly, trying to finish as fast as he could, pushed on by the Baron's fierce gaze.

Sarah kicked and clawed, nearly escaping from the Baron's clutches. He grabbed her arm and pulled her closer to his rotted, skull face.

"LEAVE HER ALONE!" I screamed.

Suddenly I felt my legs go out from under me, knocking me to the floor.

I rolled over quickly to see the hideous brother of the Baron, holding my legs with his huge hands. His eyes narrowed and his puckering mouth slid back over tiny, needle-like teeth, emitting a terrible *hissss*.

"NOOO!" I screamed, thrusting the horseshoe in front of me, sending him reeling back in horror.

Behind him, I saw all the ghosts in the room grouping together, ready to rush me, refusing to give up, *determined that the ceremony end at last.*

They filled the aisle with glowing eyes and outstretched hands.

I kicked and screamed, scrambling desperately, trying to get to my feet.

Then everyone stopped.
They stopped moving and all heads turned from me . . . to the altar.

Silence fell over the room. All eyes were locked on the altar and the three people standing there.

"No," I gasped. *Could I have been too late? Could it be over? Were they married?*

The Baron smiled and leaned over to kiss the bride, the teeth of his skull fixed into a rotted, hideous grin, a blue sparkle crackling in his eyes.

Sarah screamed "NOOOOOOOO!", and kicked him hard in the stomach.

He let her go, clutching himself.

Sarah ran from the altar and into a doorway, hidden in the alcove behind them.

"RUN! SARAH, RUN! . . . oh,no." I gulped, the realization hitting me.

My eyes turned from the Baron, cursing and clutching himself . . .

to the balcony, high overhead, jutting from the rear wall of the cathedral.

In horror, I watched Baron Oscar Bluecher run into the doorway, chasing after Sarah, screaming with rage.

Somehow I knew where they had gone. I knew where the doorway led.

It would end in the balcony.

Like before. Like with his first bride. Like the legend in the book. They would fight and they would fall from the balcony . . . to their deaths on the marble floor.

History was about to repeat itself.

22

The ghosts behind me began to fade, *their* roles in the wedding done.

All that was left was the falling . . .

and the dying.

I ran to the alcove behind the altar and into the door, following Sarah and the Baron.

As I suspected, a spiral staircase led up and up and up . . .

"To the balcony," I choked, dreading what I would find.

A scream echoed down the stairs.

"SARAH!" I cried, lunging up the stairs, as fast as I could go.

I emerged from the stairs and saw them struggling near the edge of the balcony, the room with its tiny benches spreading out far, far below.

The horrid, little skeleton clawed and shoved at Sarah, trying to push her off. Bursts of blue light erupted from its mummified skin as she tore at it, screaming.

"GET AWAY FROM HER, YOU LOUSY, BLUE BOOGER BRAIN!" I cried.

"WHAT?" he cried in surprise, turning toward me.

Sarah grabbed her opportunity. Her teeth clenched as tight as her fists. She slugged him in the stomach, doubling him over with a mighty punch.

I rushed forward, ready to knock him over the side into the room below . . .

"SARAH! RUNNNNN!" I screamed, as he stepped to the side, tripping me, sending me plunging over the balcony.

Sarah screamed as I managed to grab the railing, dangling by one arm, fifty feet over the marble floor of the cathedral.

"HELP! HEEELP!" I cried weakly, as I watched his terrible face peer over the side, the evil crackling in his eyes. His mummified fist raised above me, ready to smash my fingers.

I'd fall.

I'd DIE!

HE WAS GOING TO KILL ME!

Then with a tremendous, painful THWAK, he fell away from the railing, knocked to the floor of the balcony by my sister, Sarah.

"ALL RIGHT, SARAH!" I cheered. She didn't run! She saved me . . . at least for the moment.

With a tremendous effort, I pulled myself back up over the railing into the balcony, in time to see . . .

the Baron, his rear firmly on the floor, staring up at Sarah with absolute disbelief and humiliation, *pushed down onto his noble rear by a common girl.*

"YOU INSOLENT LITTLE PIG. WIFE OR NO, I'LL HAVE YOUR HEAD!" His eyes blazed and his arms shook in anger.

He scrambled to his withered legs with the strength of a madman, the vision of Sarah's plummeting doom gleaming in his wicked eyes.

"SARAH! LOOK OUT!" I jumped from the railing just as the Baron lunged wildly.

I knocked Sarah out of the way as he *missed her* . . .

and plunged over the railing, off the balcony, plummeting to the marble floor. . .

down
　　down,
　　　　down . . .

into the opened trunk waiting below.

The lid slammed shut, the latches locked, and a very happy young girl ghost in a white wedding gown stepped smugly to the side.

We did it.

The Baron was trapped, locked safely in the trunk by the ghost of the girl who rejected him, his first would-be wife.

Sarah and I leaned back into the balcony, relieved that it was over.

"That was a great punch, Sarah," I sighed, puffing out what felt like years of stark terror.

"You didn't do so bad yourself, Simon."

"YEAH!" We high-fived with our hands trembling from excitement, not fear.

23

We walked across the empty cathedral floor up to the ghostly girl, still standing by the locked trunk.

"Not a creature is stirring, not even a rotten, lousy, little Baron," Sarah mumbled, checking the trunk over for good measure. No way would she take a chance on that thing getting loose again. She kicked it, getting one last good jab in.

"Thank you," I said sheepishly to the ghostly girl. "I'm glad you didn't have to die this time *or* marry the creep."

"Thank *you*," she said sweetly, kissing my cheek. It felt like the puff of a cold, light breeze.

Then she was gone.

Slowly the castle around us dissolved, leaving us standing in the living room.

The trunk lay closed exactly where it was before, the wet wrapping still thrown in plastic piles to the side.

"So far, so good," I breathed in relief.

"Let's check the house," Sarah said.

The kitchen light flipped on, revealing a spotless room. Not even a scuff on the floor.

The upstairs hall table sat securely against the wall, the vase still intact.

My room had been put into perfect order, clothes neatly folded, desk neatly arranged, except for the very *bare* corkboard where my cartoons used to be.

They were probably still at Kyle's, plastered all over his upstairs hallway.

"Oh, well. You can't win 'em all," I mumbled.

The front door opened and we shoved a very poorly taped box end over end onto the doorstep. It stopped with a heavy thump, the trunk safely inside.

We stepped out into the cool, night air. It had finally stopped raining.

I drew a very nasty COOL DOG YAK face on the side of the box, and with big scrawled letters wrote:

RETURN TO SENDER!

"There," I smiled, capping my pen with an artist's pride. "My best work."

"LOOK!" Sarah yelled.

The van, the same van which had dropped the stupid trunk off in the first place, pulled into our driveway.

I could read the letters on the side of the van very clearly. They read:

FED–HEX. *If they absolutely deserve to get it overnight.*

The driver closed the door and pulled a pen out from under his beaten cap. He tapped the clicker end on his clipboard several times, approaching our doorstep.

"Oh! Hey, you kids. I'm afraid I made a wrong delivery here earlier. . . Could I . . ."

He saw the box and wrinkled his face.

"Hmmmmm. It looks all mangled. You kids didn't open it did you?"

Sarah and I looked at each other.

"Us? Oh, no. No," we mumbled, shaking our heads. A lie.

He scratched his head under his hat and grinned, checking his clipboard. "Well, that's good. Yeah, that's good. Say listen, you wouldn't know where . . . Oh, there it is, never mind. Heh, I gotta get this thing delivered."

With a huff, he picked up the box with the trunk inside, slinging it up onto his wide, strong shoulder.

With a wink, he said "Now, you kids take care."

He started back toward the van.

Whistling . . .

Then he turned and marched over to. . .

"What?" Sarah exclaimed.

"NO WAY!" I cheered.

KYLE BANNER'S HOUSE! He dropped the box off on Kyle's doorstep, knocking loudly and ringing the bell!

I couldn't believe it!

Kyle Banner was getting the deadly delivery! YES!

"Come on Simon, let's go in. Mom and Dad will be back soon."

Sarah and I gleefully turned to go back inside the house.

"Hmmm. Look at that." Sarah grinned.

Taped to the front door was a particularly nasty COOL DOG YAK cartoon. Big red letters scrawled on the bottom read:

YOU'RE DEAD MEAT,
SIMON WHITE!
Love, Kyle

"I don't think so," I laughed, pulling it down, wadding it up . . .

and closing the door.

And now
an exciting preview
of the next

STRANGE MATTER™

#10 Knightmare

by Johnny Ray Barnes, Jr.

1

"Things Are Coming to Life
at The Fairfield Museum."

That's what the banner said.

A Tyrannosaurus Rex skeleton threatened to eat the words at the end of the sentence. *Pretty silly*, I thought. The old museum had never been big enough to hold something like that. Maybe in the science building next to it, but never in the history wing.

Then I saw the scaffolding that framed the arch above the entrance stairs. Someone had taped off one of the four doorways.

"What's going on?" I asked curiously, not expecting anyone to answer.

Someone did.

"Renovation. They're putting in a back door

for you chickens to run out of when you get scared," said Kyle Banner as he passed me, horsing his way to the front of our field trip group. "Don't you know anything, Moonwalker?"

Moonwalker. My new nickname.

Even on a class trip to the museum, I couldn't get any peace. We had just stepped off the bus and already I felt depressed.

You see, when anyone in the school thinks of the name Mitchell Garrison, they think "coward". Kyle Banner seemed to always want to keep the idea fresh in everyone's heads. If not for that creep, I'd have no problems at all.

"Don't worry about him, Mitchell. He's just trying to get your goat," Keri said to me before walking ahead. She's still my friend, but it's almost like she *has* to be. She's sort of indirectly responsible for what happened, but I have to take most of the blame.

Just a month ago, I led a normal life. I had lots of friends, lots of laughs, and lots of confidence, until that day after school when Kyle Banner decided to harass Keri for not giving him the answers to that morning's English test. She and I walk home together.

He'd picked a great location to hassle us, too,

just far enough away from school grounds where no teachers could see. Unfortunately, a lot of kids take that route home, and they stopped to see what was going on. Pretty soon a crowd formed. I felt a million eyes on me, and every one of them expected me to defend myself and Keri's honor. They cheered me on, yelling for me to take a swing, to knock Kyle's block off.

But I didn't. My legs turned to jelly as Kyle's fist loomed in the air, just looking for the perfect spot to pop me. My stomach jerked nervously, and fear took control of my useless body.

I backed away from him.

In those steps, I'd earned my ticket into Fairfield Junior High's Hall of Cowardice, and Kyle dubbed me "Moonwalker", after Michael Jackson's famous dance move. To my horror, the moniker stuck, and now that's what everyone calls me.

But the skirmish didn't end there, at least not Kyle's part of it. Trey Porter stepped up from the crowd and did exactly what I should've done. He looked Kyle square in the eyes, and told him if it was a fight he was looking for, he'd found it. The bully sized him up, and looked like he thought Trey could back up his threats. Kyle retreated, but he'd completed his mission.

He destroyed me, socially. Even though I backed down, having Trey take care of the mess for me made me look even worse. I thought I'd never live that day down, the most humiliating one of my life. Little did I know how soon that would change.

"Hey, Mitch, are you reliving that day in your head again? You're letting that experience scar your psyche, pal," said Howard. Howard Peel's the only other person besides Keri who will talk to me. He says he's got big plans on how to get me back in good graces with the rest of the class.

"Howard, do you even know what a psyche is?" I asked him. His use of the word smelled of current dictionary perusal.

"Sure. It's the soul or spirit. Do you know what the Deschaul Exhibit is?" Howard threw his question right back at me.

"No. What is it?" I asked him as the class started to move through the three open doors.

"It's the big Medieval exhibit old man Deschaul's had hauled to Fairfield from France. It's supposed to be kickin'."

"What's that got to do with the soul or

spirit?" I asked.

"Everything. It's got everything to do with repairing *your psyche*. I've got a plan, man."

"Huh?" I asked, but Howard didn't say another word, and we continued through the door.

Our teacher, Mrs. Spearman, hushed the class as we walked into the foyer, which had been expanded on each side. Part of the renovation, I guessed. I found that a little silly, too. Any time they added any major exhibit at all, the museum had to be renovated. It had originally been the old town hall. When Fairfield's new City Hall went up in the late 60's, they converted this building to hold all of the town treasures. At any rate, the more they put in the place, the bigger it got.

"All right, class. I think you all know Mr. Deschaul."

Wow. Mr. René Deschaul himself had offered to show our class around. Everyone knew him as one of the richest men in Fairfield, and also as director of the town's History Museum and Science Center. I'd only seen him in the paper, though. He looked a lot older in person, with gray hair and big, puffy eyes. He kept tugging at his tight shirt collar that pinched the fat around his neck. When he shuffled his feet, I noticed his stumpy legs and realized that he couldn't be much taller than I am. All of his moving about simply let the class clue in on his nervousness. He wanted to be somewhere else, doing anything else.

"I'll be honest with you, kids. If I had known you were coming today, I would've made Mrs. Handle, our regular guide, reschedule her vacation. But since she's in Bermuda and I'm not, I guess I'll have to run you through some of the new exhibits we've acquired here at the museum."

Hands instantly shot into the air with questions hanging below them. Mr. Deschaul smiled crookedly and took the first three.

"Are there drink machines in the museum now?" Hank Dunk asked in his usual dimwitted manner.

"No," Mr. Deschaul answered.

Then Keri asked, "So there are no dinosaur bones like the banner outside leads you to believe?"

"No, that banner was designed by a free-lance graphic artist who was not on staff and not familiar with what the museum contained. We didn't pay him for the job either, I believe. One more question. Yes, you young man . . ." He pointed to Howard.

"Yes, sir. Are we going to see the Medieval exhibit today?"

Mr. Deschaul's expression grew serious. "Everything in that exhibit's being checked right now and probably won't be set up for another week. But you kids can feel free to come back and see it with your parents. They'll have to pay full price, but you can get in for half of that."

With that questionable welcome, Mr. Deschaul led the entire class to the first room of historical findings.

That's when Howard grabbed the back of my shirt to stop me.

"What is it?" I asked.

"Come on, let's go," he grinned.

"Where?" I asked.

"I think I know where the Medieval exhibit is. We're going to sneak in and see it. Let's go." His eyes had that happy dog look in them.

"Mrs. Spearman will murder us," I told him.

"Mrs. Spearman will never know. We'll be in and out in less than a minute."

"I don't know . . ."

"Come on, Mitch," Howard urged. "It'll be

cool! And when everyone finds out you saw it, they'll think you're cool!"

That sold me.

We backed away from the group, and quickly lost ourselves down one of the long, dark side halls.

If I had known then what awaited us, I never would have followed.

About the Authors

Marty M. Engle and **Johnny Ray Barnes Jr.**, graduates of the Art Institute of Atlanta, are the creators, writers, designers and illustrators of the **Strange Matter**™ series and the **Strange Matter**™ World Wide Web page.

Their interests and expertise range from state of the art 3-D computer graphics and interactive multi-media, to books and scripts (television and motion picture).

Marty lives in La Jolla, California with his wife Jana and twin terror pets, Polly and Oreo.

Johnny Ray lives in Tierrasanta, California and spends every free moment with his fiancée, Meredith.

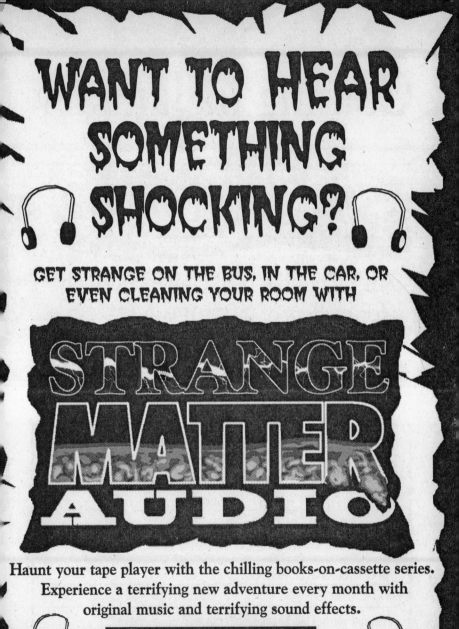

CONTINUE THE ADVENTURE...

with the StrangeMatter™ library.
Experience a terrifying new
StrangeMatter™ adventure every month.

#1 No Substitutions
#2 Midnight Game
#3 Driven to Death
#4 A Place to Hide
#5 The Last One In

#6 Bad Circuits
#7 Fly the Unfriendly Skies
#8 Frozen Dinners
#9 Deadly Delivery
#10 KnightMare

Available where you buy books.

FEARSOME FACTS

💀 The ghosts of "Deadly Delivery" were based in part on the documented sightings and historic hauntings of Glamis castle in Angus, Scotland. There are many books about these and other ghosts at your local library.

💀 According to some researchers, ghosts are not always visible and do not always appear in human form. Some may manifest as cold spots on the floor, others as ghostly balls of light or even as disturbances in the air, noticeable only by sensitive equipment.

💀 Some researchers believe that ghosts are not the spectral spirits of people, but are instead magnetic recordings picked up by surrounding objects and replayed over and over in the air, like a videotape recorder.

ARE YOU A STRANGER?

If so, get busy and send us your

Cool Drawings

or

SCARY STORIES

and you may see your work in ...

THE **STRANGERS**

N E W S L E T T E R

Send to your fiends at:
STRANGERS ART & STORIES
Montage Publications
9808 Waples St.
San Diego, California 92121